CYCLOPS

CYCLOPS

WRITTEN AND ILLUSTRATED BY
LEONARD EVERETT FISHER

HOLIDAY HOUSE / NEW YORK

SPAIN

The following sources were consulted by the author in retelling this ancient Greek myth:

Bullfinch, T. *Mythology*. New York: Random House, Inc., Modern Library.

Ceram, C. W. *Gods, Graves, and Scholars*. New York: Alfred Knopf, Inc., 1956.

Graves, R. *The Greek Myths*. Volume II, New York: George Braziller, Inc., 1959.

Hamilton, E. *Mythology*. Boston: Little, Brown & Co., Inc., 1940.

Lattimore, R. (translator). *The Odyssey of Homer*. New York: HarperCollins, 1940.

For Margery Cuyler

Copyright © 1991 by Leonard Everett Fisher
ALL RIGHTS RESERVED
PRINTED IN THE UNITED STATES OF AMERICA
FIRST EDITION

LIBRARY OF CONGRESS CATALOGING-IN-PUBLICATION DATA

FISHER, LEONARD EVERETT.
CYCLOPS / WRITTEN AND ILLUSTRATED BY LEONARD EVERETT FISHER.—
1ST ED.
P. CM.
INCLUDES BIBLIOGRAPHICAL REFERENCES.
SUMMARY: DESCRIBES THE ENCOUNTER BETWEEN THE CYCLOPS POLYPHEMUS
AND ODYSSEUS AND HIS MEN AFTER THE END OF THE TROJAN WAR.
ISBN 0-8234-0891-4
1. POLYPHEMUS (GREEK MYTHOLOGY)—JUVENILE LITERATURE.
2. CYCLOPES (GREEK MYTHOLOGY)—JUVENILE LITERATURE.
[1. POLYPHEMUS (GREEK MYTHOLOGY) 2. CYCLOPES (GREEK MYTHOLOGY)
3. ODYSSEUS (GREEK MYTHOLOGY) 4. MYTHOLOGY, GREEK.] I. TITLE.
BL820.C83F57   1991   90-29317   CIP   AC
398.21—DC20

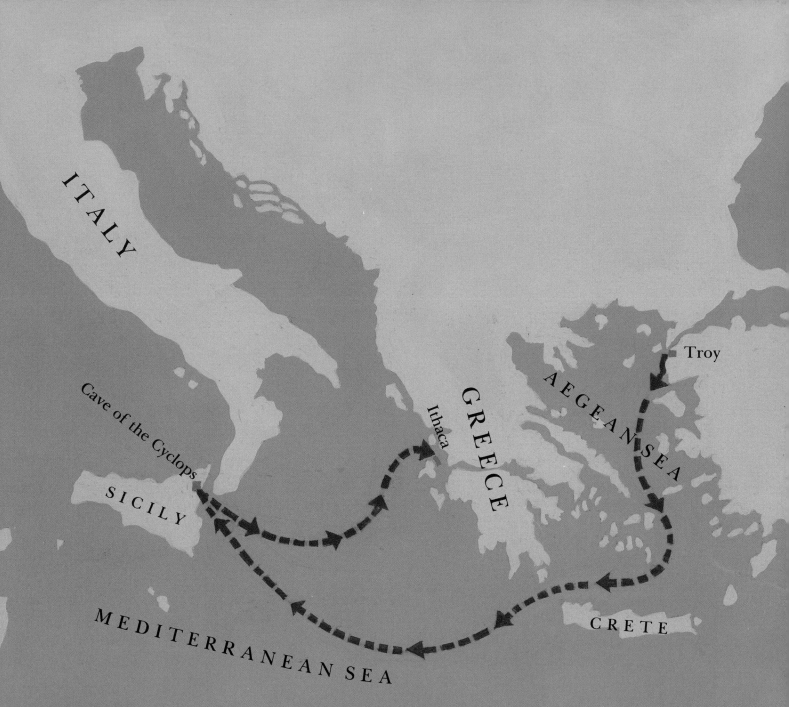

ITALY

Cave of the Cyclops

SICILY

GREECE

Ithaca

Troy

AEGEAN SEA

CRETE

MEDITERRANEAN SEA

INTRODUCTION

Homer, an ancient Greek poet, wrote about a race of
monsters called the Cyclopes. They were ugly, mean
giants who had one hideous eye in the center of their
foreheads. They lived in caves on the island of Sicily,
where they tended sheep and goats and made thun-
derbolts for Zeus, king of the gods. In his long poem,
The Odyssey, Homer told about the wanderings of the
Greek general, Odysseus, and his men. They out-
witted the Cyclops, Polyphemus, after becoming
stranded on the giant's island.

AFRICA

Odysseus and his Greek army had been fighting for ten years in a faraway city called Troy. At last they conquered the city and sailed for Ithaca, their island home.

The gods were angry at the warriors. The Greeks had dragged Princess Cassandra from her temple in Troy. The temple was a holy and peaceful place, not meant for violent acts. The gods felt that the men should be punished for their deed. They sent a fierce storm that battered Odysseus's ship and blew it far off course.

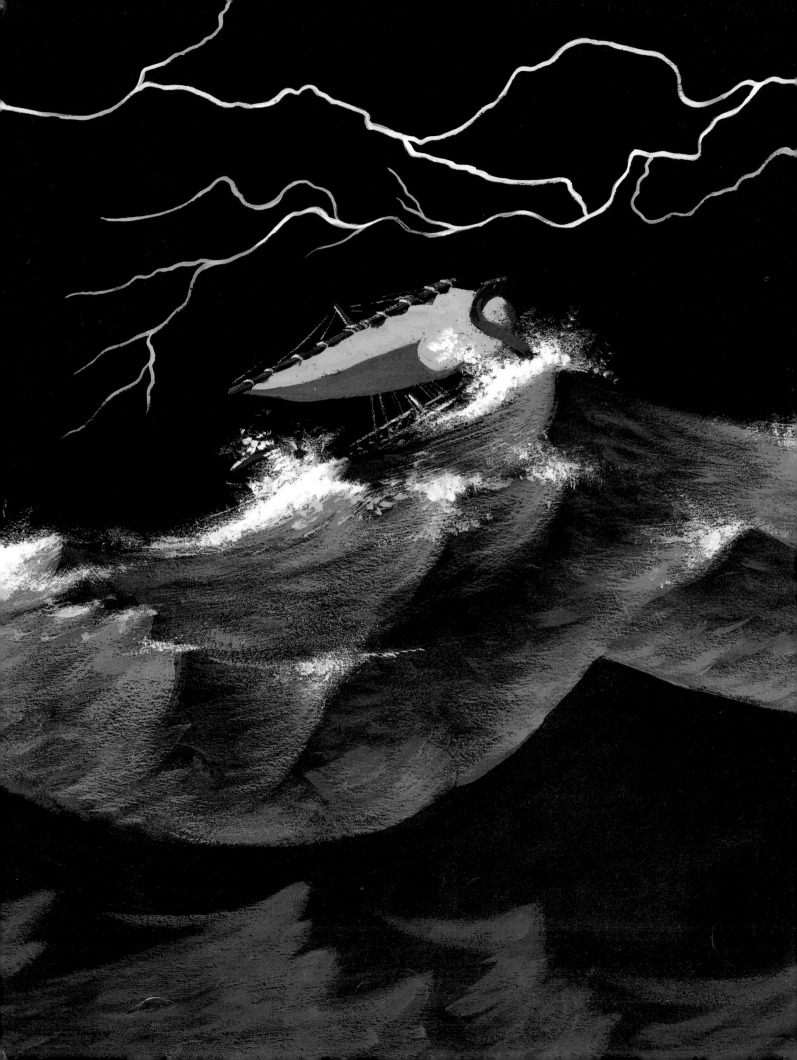

Odysseus and his men finally landed on the shore of an island. Great mountains soared above them and disappeared into misty clouds high in the sky. Sharp cliffs dropped into the crashing sea. Low-lying, sandy hills hid fields and valleys beyond.

"Make fast the lines!" Odysseus shouted above the roar of the breaking surf. "We'll stay here until the storm is over."

Exhausted from their journey, the warriors rested and made plans to search for food.

Odysseus took twelve of his men and set out over the hills. They soon discovered a vast cave with a gigantic stone at the entrance. They went inside, where they found hundreds of bleating baby lambs and goats. In the flickering firelight, they saw tubs of milk, stacks of cheeses, piles of meats, sacks of vegetables, and baskets of fruits. No one was there.

"What a storehouse!" Odysseus pointed out. "I'm sure whoever lives here wouldn't mind if we had something to eat. When he returns, we can explain who we are and offer him a gift of wine."

The men began to feast, but as they were enjoying their first good meal in weeks, the ground trembled. A shadow fell across the cave entrance, blocking the outside light. A giant as big and thick as a small mountain slowly crawled into the cave, driving a herd of sheep ahead of him. Once inside, he pulled the great stone boulder across the entrance.

"We are trapped," groaned one of the warriors.

Slowly, the huge creature turned. Odysseus and his men looked up and saw one horrible eye in the middle of the monster's forehead. There was no place to hide. The terrified Greeks pressed themselves against the wall of the cave.

The giant turned toward the cowering men. His huge eye gleamed in the dancing light. "Who are you and why are you here?" he roared.

"We are Greek warriors," answered Odysseus. "We won a victory over the city of Troy and are on our way home. We are here because our ship was blown off course. Our great god Zeus protects us. No harm will come to you," he continued. "We only ask that you share your food with us, and that you accept our gift of wine."

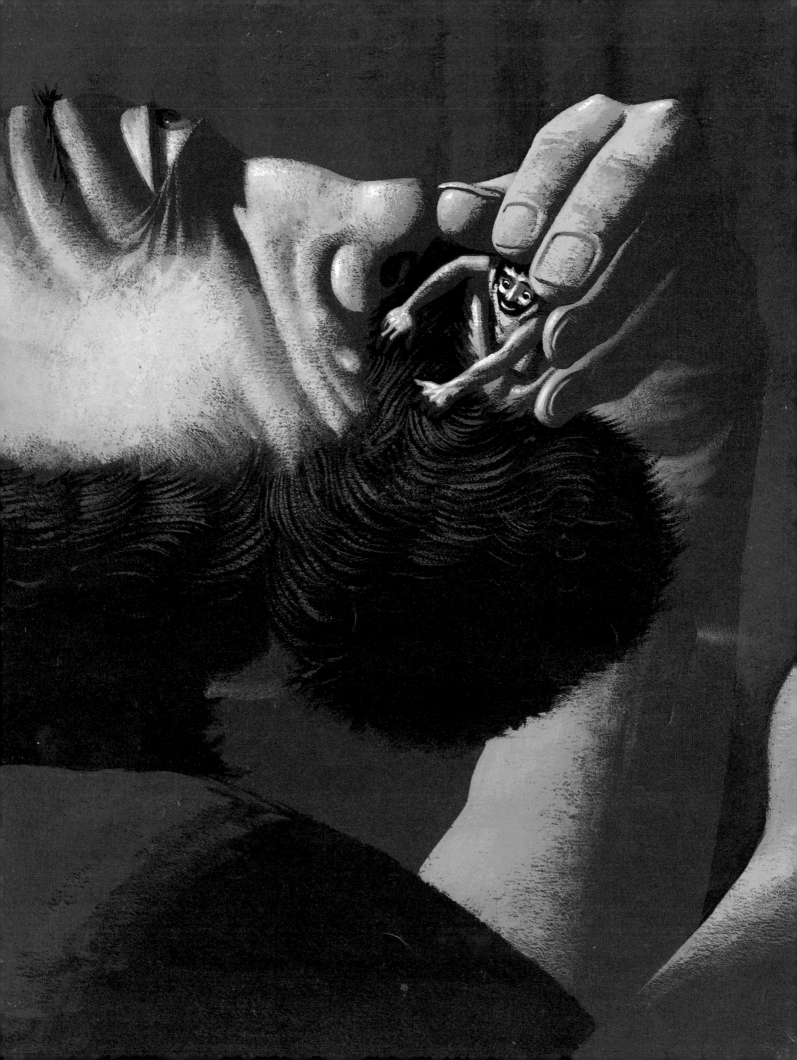

"I have no fear of Zeus!" the one-eyed giant jeered. "I, Polyphemus, am bigger and stronger than any god! or any man!" He reached into the group, scooped up two men, and ate them. Odysseus watched in horror as the Cyclops washed his dinner down with one great gulp of goat's milk, and fell asleep.

"We are doomed if we do not move the boulder blocking the entrance," Odysseus whispered. The terrified men tried but were unable to budge the stone. Too afraid to sleep, Odysseus stayed awake all night, trying to think of a plan of escape.

Polyphemus awoke at daybreak. Odysseus and his men watched in dread as he rose to milk the goats.

When the Cyclops finished, he reached out for his morning meal. He quickly ate two more of the men. Then he washed them down with goat's milk and pushed the entrance boulder aside. Driving his sheep before him, the one-eyed monster left the cave. He pushed the stone back into place, leaving the Greeks trapped inside.

While the giant watched his sheep under a bright and sunny sky, Odysseus told the eight men who were left the plan he'd thought of the night before. They began to plot their escape.

Searching the cave for a weapon, they came across a huge log. Odysseus ordered his men to make it into a stake by chiseling a point at one end. When that was done, they hid the stake in the deep shadows of the cave and waited for Polyphemus.

Late that afternoon, the giant returned. He drove his sheep into the cave and pulled the boulder back into place behind him. Then he squatted on the cave floor and snatched two more of Odysseus's men for his dinner.

Before the monster could gulp down some goat's milk, Odysseus stepped forward. With the screams of the victims still ringing in his ears, he approached the monster.

"You must taste our wine, great Polyphemus," Odysseus offered. "It is delicious and will warm your heart."

Polyphemus grabbed a goatskin and began to drink. After a few gulps, he turned to Odysseus and asked, "What is your name?"

"Noman," Odysseus replied, not wanting to tell the giant his real name.

"Noman, is it? Well, Noman, I shall have you for dinner one of these days!"

The giant poured the last of the wine down his throat and fell asleep in a drunken stupor.

Odysseus and the six remaining Greeks took the stake from its hiding place. They heated the pointed end in the fire. With all their strength, they rammed it into Polyphemus's only eye. "Aaagh!" cried the giant. Blinded, he tried to grab his attackers. But Odysseus and his men jumped out of the way.

"I'll get you in the morning," the blinded giant bellowed. "You cannot escape without moving the boulder. You are not strong enough for that!"

Then he quit thrashing about, rolled over on his back, and fell asleep.

During the night, the men each tied three sheep together. Then they waited for morning. At sunrise, Polyphemus awoke, blind and roaring with rage. He tried and failed to catch one of the men for breakfast. "Just you wait!" he growled. "If you try to escape on the backs of my sheep, I'll grab you!"

He pushed aside the entrance stone and let his sheep out. As the sheep passed from the cave, Polyphemus blindly felt their backs. Little did he know that underneath, clinging to the sheeps' shaggy wool, were Odysseus and his men.

Free at last, the Greeks raced back to the beach and joined the rest of the crew. They pushed their boat into the water. As they rowed away from the shore, Odysseus shouted out to the Cyclops.

"Polyphemus, your guests are free and have gone to sea! We are no longer yours for breakfast and dinner! You have been properly punished for your cruelty."

Polyphemus tore the log from his eye and threw it in the direction of the voice. He tore a piece of the mountain from his island and heaved it into the sea. Its great splash nearly swamped the boat. But a brisk wind carried the men from the island and the Cyclops.

Polyphemus sat at the water's edge. His prisoners had escaped. The stories they would tell of his defeat would last forever. Who would ever fear the blinded Cyclops, Polyphemus, again? His great might was no match for the clever Odysseus and his brave crew.

"Who did this to you, Polyphemus?" asked the other Cyclopes.

"Noman," replied the wounded giant, reciting the name that Odysseus had given instead of his own.

"If no man did this foul deed, then you have been struck by Zeus," they declared, "the god of us all!"

And they left him to his misery.